HANDEL

and the Famous Sword Swallower of Halle

BY *Bryna Stevens*

ILLUSTRATED BY *Ruth Tietjen Councell*

PHILOMEL BOOKS
New York

To my piano student Adam Cockman,
who always loved reading about George Frederick Handel
and the Famous Sword Swallower of Halle
— B.S.

To my mother
— R.T.C.

PEOPLE IN HALLE, Germany, were upset. George Handel, their old barber-surgeon had decided to remarry! Sixty was too old to take on a new wife, people said, especially since his new wife was only thirty-two. But George Handel wasn't a person who spent much time worrying what people thought, and so in April 1683 he married pretty Dorothea Taust.

Now, sixty was considered old in 1683 because most people then didn't live much past fifty, but at sixty George Handel was the town's best barber-surgeon. He didn't seem very old even though his long wavy hair was white and startling against the black satin coat he always wore. He was tall and handsome for sixty, and very rich. In fact, he lived in the biggest house in town, which is why he wanted to remarry. (Living alone in that big house was just too lonely.)

Two years later a son, George Frederick, was born, and Dorothea's unmarried sister, Anna Taust, moved in to help take care of the new baby.

Actually, if Anna Taust had had any other place to go she wouldn't have moved in because she never got along well with George Handel, Senior. (Both of Anna Taust's parents had died of the plague, which is why she had no home. George Handel's first wife had died of the plague, too. In fact, half of Halle's citizens had died of the plague. George Handel caught the plague too, but he got better.)

What Anna Taust disliked most about George Handel, Senior, was that he didn't like music. In fact, George Handel, Senior, tried hard to keep music out of his family's life altogether. When the evening bells from nearby Church of Our Beloved Lady rang through the town, George Handel, Senior, shut the windows. When choirs and street musicians roamed about Halle, singing hymns and folk tunes for money, George Handel, Senior, paid them to stop. When royal princes held private concerts in their homes and George Handel, Senior, was invited, he refused as many invitations as he dared. Indeed, when Anna Taust wanted to sing to her baby nephew, she had to pick times when George Handel, Senior, was busy in his barber shop.

Now, men in most barber shops in the late 1600s gathered round to sing and make merry. In fact, that's how barber-shop quartets began, but there wasn't any music in George Handel, Senior's shop because he thought music was a lot of foolishness and a waste of time. (There wasn't much haircutting in his shop, either. Blood-stained bandages outside his shop told everyone in Halle that he was a barber-surgeon and not just an ordinary barber. Barber-surgeons, not doctors, pulled teeth, mended broken bones, fixed boils and bled people, which was thought back then to cure diseases.)

But Aunt Anna was stubborn, just as stubborn as George Handel, Senior. Even though he tried to keep music away from his son, Aunt Anna managed to surround her nephew with music. On Sunday mornings she took him to the Church of Our Beloved Lady, where they listened to Friedrich Zachau (pronounced *za*-cow), the church organist, play the organ. Sometimes when the music swelled, the huge stone church shook with sound and it seemed to George Frederick that it might burst. (George Handel, Senior, probably didn't think about the music at church; he was just happy that George Frederick was learning about God.)

Sunday afternoons, George Frederick and Aunt Anna went to the park near Halle. On spring and summer Sundays it was like a carnival. Jugglers juggled bright colored balls, apples and oranges and anything else that was handy. Magicians put on magic shows. And best of all, traveling musicians sang and played their lutes and guitars, and sometimes Gypsies in bright colored skirts danced. George Frederick loved the music and never wanted to go home. (George Handel, Senior, very likely didn't mind. He was growing older and probably appreciated some peace and quiet.)

But one day George Handel, Senior, found George Frederick playing a toy drum, a gift from Aunt Anna, and that simply was too much. Neither George Frederick's tears nor Aunt Anna's pleading kept the drum from the fire. Music was not allowed in the barber-surgeon's house, and musical toys would not be tolerated either!

But Aunt Anna wasn't a person who gave up easily. Soon after, when George Frederick was only seven, she whispered that she had a surprise. George Frederick eagerly followed her up three flights of wooden stairs to the attic. And there in a corner stood a little clavichord. (A clavichord is smaller than a piano and has a delicate, tinkling sound. Aunt Anna had wrapped its strings with cloth so it would sound even quieter.) She was certain George Handel, Senior, would never be able to hear the music from three floors below.

Quickly, George Frederick sat down at the clavichord. He struck a few keys. Then he played more and more notes until the attic was filled with his music. Aunt Anna just listened proudly.

Day after day George Frederick rushed home from the *Gymnasium* to play his little clavichord. (*Gymnasium*, pronounced gim-*nah*-zee-um, the *g* hard as in "gift," was the name for school in Germany back in the 1600s.) At first, George Frederick played melodies he had heard before, but soon he began making up his own tunes. How Aunt Anna wished her young nephew could take lessons. Still, George Frederick was happy. Each day he practiced his clavichord upstairs while his father practiced surgery downstairs.

USUALLY, GEORGE FREDERICK did not see the people who came into his father's shop. He kept himself busy studying Greek and Latin for school, and playing his clavichord in the attic. Besides, it wasn't pleasant to see people hobbling along in pain when something needed to be fixed. But surely he would have stared in horror if he'd seen Andreas Rudloff, a young boy who had swallowed a knife, come into his father's shop.

The case of Andreas Rudloff was most unusual. At sixteen years of age, Andreas should have known better than to run with a knife in his mouth. But he didn't, and suddenly he tripped and fell. The stag-horn-handled knife plunged deep into his throat, too deep to reach.

A doctor had Andreas drink warm beer and olive oil, hoping these would loosen the blade. The warm beer and olive oil did not work. Neither did the medicine the doctor thought might dissolve the blade. When the doctor didn't know what else to try, Andreas' mother sent for George Handel, Senior. But the barber-surgeon shook his head, too. He didn't know what else to do either.

During the next year, George Frederick continued playing his clavichord, and Andreas Rudloff continued to live with the knife inside him. When a lump appeared on his chest, his mother became frightened. She thought a boil was growing on her son's heart.

She sent for the barber-surgeon again. George Handel, Senior, studied the lump. He didn't think it was a boil. When he opened the lump, he stared at the tip of the knife blade coming through. He bored a hole in the tip, tied a silk thread through it, and little by little inched the knife out.

After that, Andreas Rudloff was always known as the Famous Sword Swallower of Halle. People were amazed at what George Handel, Senior, had done. His fame spread far and wide and young George Frederick was known as the son of a very famous man.

Even Duke Johann Adolph I at Weissenfels (pronounced *vie*-sen-fels) heard about George Handel, Senior, and the Famous Sword Swallower of Halle. He sent for the famous barber-surgeon at once. He decided that no one but George Handel would treat him and the members of his court. (In fact, the duke knew George Handel, Senior, because he had been the duke's father's barber-surgeon before he and his court moved to Weissenfels.)

GEORGE FREDERICK made the long, dusty trip to the castle in a carriage with his father. George Frederick had reason to be excited. There was the Augustusburg castle to see, there was George Christian, his nephew ten years older than himself whom he had never met, and there was the music at the castle that he'd heard so much about. (It was said that the Duke of Weissenfels was a great lover of music.)

Soon after arriving, the barber-surgeon became busy with the duke, and George Christian showed George Frederick about the castle. Huge chandeliers that glittered like diamonds hung from the ceilings. Paintings in thick gold frames hung from the walls.

Then George Frederick heard some music pouring out from a room. When he peeked inside, he saw a room that looked like a church. Sunlight glowed through stained-glass windows and way up front sat a man playing one of the biggest organs George Frederick had ever seen. (Its pipes nearly touched the ceiling!) Wonderful music filled the room. George Frederick and George Christian sat down quietly and listened.

When the music ended, George Christian brought George Frederick forward down the long, long room to meet the organist. When the organist learned that George Frederick knew how to play the clavichord, he asked George Frederick if he'd like to try playing the organ.

He did!

George Frederick climbed up on the organ bench. His legs were too short to reach the long pedals so he just played the organ with his fingers. Soon, once more, the music swelled and filled the room. George Christian and the organist were amazed at how fast young George Frederick's fingers moved over the keys. Neither one had ever heard an eight-year-old child play so well. (They were stunned even more when they heard that George Frederick had never taken any lessons.)

The duke must be told about this amazing child at once. The organist rushed to find the duke.

The duke listened, then sent for George Handel, Senior. The duke urged the barber-surgeon to let his son study music. George Handel, Senior, refused (respectfully, of course, because the duke was a very important man).

The duke spoke again. "Such talent can only come from God!" he said. "It would be a sin against God not to let your son study music!"

George Handel, Senior, was quiet. People before had begged him to let George Frederick study music, but no one had ever suggested that he'd been sinning against God by saying no! Finally, he said yes.

Before George Frederick and his father left the castle, the duke filled George Frederick's pockets with gold coins.

"More will be coming, if you practice every day," the duke said.

George Frederick began studying music as soon as they returned to Halle, which of course made Aunt Anna very happy. Friedrich Zachau, the organist at church, turned out to be a very fine teacher. He taught George Frederick how to play the harpsichord (an instrument something like a clavichord), the organ and the violin. He taught him how to compose music, too.

And sometimes when Friedrich Zachau was very busy, George Frederick played the organ in his place at church. And now as young George Frederick played, organ music swelled through the huge stone church, thrilling listeners with majestic sound. George Frederick, too, was filled with joy, the joy of creation, the miracle of music.

The barber-surgeon still didn't like music, but in time he grew to be proud of his talented son. During the next thirty-two years George Frederick Handel composed over two hundred pieces of fine music for the organ, orchestra and for people to sing.

No one can be certain, of course, but if it hadn't been for Aunt Anna, the small clavichord she brought him, and the Famous Sword Swallower of Halle, George Frederick Handel might never have become a musician at all.

AUTHOR'S NOTE

VERY LITTLE is actually known about George Frederick Handel's childhood. That is because no one knew he was going to become a famous musician when he grew up. There are no diaries or letters to refer to. By the time George Handel did become famous, people who had known him as a child were no longer living. Most of the information about his childhood is based on a biography by John Mainwaring, first published in 1760, a year after Handel's death. Some people wonder if everything in Mainwaring's story is true. Did Aunt Anna really hide a clavichord in the attic? they ask. Yet George Handel, Senior, was a barber-surgeon, and he did remove a knife from Andreas Rudloff's chest. (Andreas became a barber-surgeon in the army when he got older.)

People also wonder if George Handel, Senior, really hated music so much, and if so, why. Some people claim the barber-surgeon was simply a practical man who wanted his son to have a career more secure than music.

What is certain is that George Frederick Handel became a world-beloved musician, the composer of the music for such classics as the *Messiah* and "Joy to the World."

REFERENCES

Coxe, William. *Anecdotes of George Frederic Handel and John Christopher Smith.* New York: Da Capo Press, 1979.

Flower, Newman. *George Frederic Handel: His Personality and His Times.* London: Cassell, 1959.

Landon, H. C. Robbins. *Handel and His World.* London: Weidenfeld & Nicolson, 1984.

Mainwaring, John. *Memoirs of the Life of the Late George Frederic Handel.* Amsterdam: Frits A. M. Knuf, 1964. (Original edition London, 1760).

Rackwitz, Werner, and Helmut Steffens. *George Frideric Handel.* Leipzig: Veb, 1962.

Text copyright © 1990 by Bryna Stevens. Illustrations copyright © 1990 by Ruth Tietjen Councell Published in 1990 by Philomel Books, a division of The Putnam & Grosset Group, 200 Madison Avenue, New York, NY 10016. All rights reserved. Published simultaneously in Canada. Printed in Hong Kong by South China Printing Co. (1988) Ltd. Book design by Kathleen Westray

Library of Congress Cataloging-in-Publication Data
Stevens, Bryna. Handel and the famous sword swallower of Halle / written by Bryna Stevens; illustrated by Ruth Tietjin Councell. p. cm. Summary: Relates how a determined aunt and a boy who swallowed a knife made it possible for young George Frederick Handel to study music despite his father's strong objections. 1. Handel, George Frideric, 1685–1759 — Childhood and youth — Juvenile literature. 2. Composers — Biography — Juvenile literature. 3. Rudloff, Andreas. [1. Handel, George Frideric, 1685–1759. 2. Composers.] I. Councell, Ruth Tietjen, ill. II. Title. ML3930.H25D66   1988 87-32438 CIP MN AC 780'.92'4 — dc19 ISBN 0-399-21548-4

First Impression